Parents and Caregivers,

Stone Arch Readers are designed to provide enjoyable reading experiences, as well as opportunities to develop vocabulary, literacy skills, and comprehension. Here are a few ways to support your beginning reader:

• Talk with your child about the ideas addressed in the story.

• Discuss each illustration, mentioning the characters, where they are, and what they are doing.

• Read with expression, pointing to each word. You may want to read the whole story through and then revisit parts of the story to ensure that the meanings of words or phrases are understood.

• Talk about why the character did what he or she did and what your child would do in that situation.

• Help your child connect with characters and events in the story.

Remember, reading with your child should be fun, not forced. Each moment spent reading with your child is a priceless investment in his or her literacy life.

Gail Saunders-Smith, Ph.D.

Stone Arch Readers

are published by Stone Arch Books
a Capstone Imprint
1710 Roe Crest Drive
North Mankato, Minnesota 56003
www.capstonepub.com

Copyright © 2014 by Stone Arch Books

Library of Congress Cataloging-in-Publication Data
Crow, Melinda Melton.
Rocky and Daisy take a vacation / by Melinda Melton Crow ; illustrated by Eva Sassin.
p. cm. — (Stone Arch readers: My two dogs)
Summary: Their family is going away without them, and Rocky and Daisy are apprehensive
about spending a week at a kennel.
ISBN 978-1-4342-6008-6 (library binding) — ISBN 978-1-4342-6202-8 (pbk.)
1. Dogs—Juvenile fiction. 2. Kennels—Juvenile fiction. [1. Dogs—Fiction. 2. Kennels—Fiction.]
I. Sassin, Eva, ill. II. Title.
PZ7.C88536Rqm 2013
813.6—dc23   2012047189

Reading Consultants:
Gail Saunders-Smith, Ph.D.
Melinda Melton Crow, M.Ed.
Laurie K. Holland, Media Specialist

Printed in China by Nordica.
0413/CA21300422
032013
007226NORDF13

Take a Vacation

by **Melinda Melton Crow**

illustrated by **Eva Sassin**

STONE ARCH BOOKS

a capstone imprint

MY TWO DOGS

I'm Owen, and these are Rocky and Daisy, my two dogs.

ROCKY LIKES:

- Chasing squirrels

- Playing with other dogs

- Chewing things

- Running with me when I
ride my bike

DAISY LIKES:

- Playing ball

- Listening to stories

- Resting on the furniture

- Eating yummy treats

Rocky and Daisy loved their
family. They loved their home.
And they loved their friend
Owen.

"We are going on vacation soon," said Owen.

"Oh, boy!" shouted Rocky. Rocky and Daisy liked to go places. They barked and wagged their tails.

"Sorry," said Mom. "We are going on an airplane. You cannot come with us this time."

Daisy lay down and covered her ears. Rocky put his head on Owen's lap.

"Please?" Rocky begged.

Dad shook his head. "I'm sorry," he said.

"You will have your own vacation," said Owen. "You will go to the kennel."

Rocky and Daisy had never
been to the kennel. They were
not sure they would like it there.

"Don't worry," said Owen.
"You will like it, I promise."

Owen packed his suitcase. He packed a few things for Rocky and Daisy, too.

Owen told Rocky and Daisy about the kennel.

"There is a fun playground," he said. "You will have comfy beds. You can even watch animal shows on TV."

It sounded fun, but Daisy was still worried.

At the kennel, Owen said good-bye to his dogs. "We will be back in one week," he said.

Rocky and Daisy were sad to
see Owen leave. But they were
happy to be together.

A nice man showed Rocky
and Daisy to their room. Rocky
spotted a bunk bed.

"I call the top bunk!" shouted
Rocky. He jumped up on top.

"You can have it," said Daisy. "I'm afraid of high places."

"Cool!" said Rocky.

Rocky and Daisy ran outside.
They saw a pool with sprinklers.

"Let's go swimming!" yelled
Rocky.

"Race you to the pool," said
Daisy.

After their swim, Rocky and
Daisy looked at the playground.

There were places to jump
and climb. There was room to
run. There were balls to chase.

Best of all, there were lots of dogs to play with. There were big dogs, little dogs, black dogs, brown dogs, and even spotted dogs!

Rocky and Daisy played all
afternoon. They were tired and
happy.

Rocky and Daisy went back to their room. "I'm hungry," cried Daisy. A man brought bowls of food and water.

After they ate, it was time for
bed. "I can't wait to play again
tomorrow," said Rocky.

Rocky and Daisy played with
their friends every day.

They dreamed of Owen and their family every night.

They missed them, but they were not lonely. The week went by very fast.

Soon Rocky and Daisy saw a familiar face. It was Owen!

"It's time to go home," said Owen.

Rocky and Daisy ran and
jumped all over Owen. They
licked his face. "I missed you,"
said Owen.

At home, Rocky and Daisy curled up with Owen on the couch. "It was fun at the kennel," said Rocky.

"But it's good to be home,"
said Daisy.

THE END

STORY WORDS

kennel   bunk   familiar

comfy   sprinklers   couch

Total Word Count: 468

READ MORE
ROCKY AND DAISY ADVENTURES!